In the **Beginner Reader** level,  ed in previous steps and introduc

ar or ur ow oi er

Special features:

Phonically decodable text
builds reading confidence

Short sentences with
simple language

The sun sets as the cows finish the song.

Barn Owl is not sad at all.

How are you now, Barn Owl?

I am better! Hoot!

Repetition of
sounds in
different words

Practice of
words that
cannot be
sounded out

14

15

Summary page
to reinforce
learning

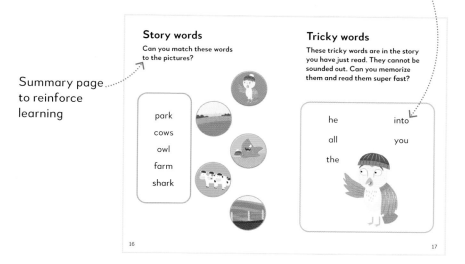

Story words

Can you match these words
to the pictures?

park
cows
owl
farm
shark

Tricky words

These tricky words are in the story
you have just read. They cannot be
sounded out. Can you memorize
them and read them super fast?

he   into
all   you
the

16

17

Ladybird

Educational Consultants: Geraldine Taylor and James Clements
Phonics and Book Banding Consultant: Kate Ruttle

LADYBIRD BOOKS

UK | USA | Canada | Ireland | Australia
India | New Zealand | South Africa

Ladybird Books is part of the Penguin Random House group of companies
whose addresses can be found at global.penguinrandomhouse.com.

www.penguin.co.uk   www.puffin.co.uk   www.ladybird.co.uk

First published 2020
This edition published 2024
001

Written by Claire Smith
Text copyright © Ladybird Books Ltd, 2020, 2024
Illustrations by Dean Gray
Illustrations copyright © Ladybird Books Ltd, 2020, 2024

Printed in China

The authorized representative in the EEA is Penguin Random House Ireland,
Morrison Chambers, 32 Nassau Street, Dublin D02 YH68

A CIP catalogue record for this book is available from the British Library

ISBN: 978-0-241-56436-3

All correspondence to:
Ladybird Books
Penguin Random House Children's
One Embassy Gardens, 8 Viaduct Gardens, London SW11 7BW

Barn Owl

Written by Claire Smith
Illustrated by Dean Gray

Barn Owl is ill.
He can not hoot.

Barn Owl is sad.

Ow!
It hurts!

In the park, he sees
Lars the shark.

A-tish-oo!

Good morning,
Barn Owl.

Lars has a hat for Barn Owl!

Barn Owl is less sad now.

On the farm, he sees
the cows.

The cows turn and chat.
How can Barn Owl get better?

A-tish-oo!

Barn Owl gets into bed.
The cows sing.

The duck joins in, too!
Barn Owl naps.

The sun sets as the cows finish the song.

How are you now, Barn Owl?

Barn Owl is not sad at all.

I am better! Hoot!

Story words

Can you match these words
to the pictures?

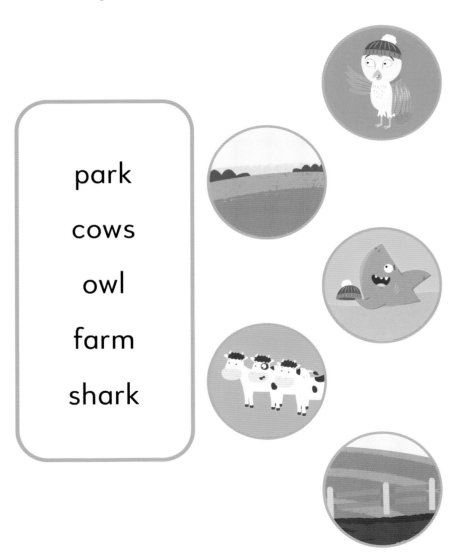

park

cows

owl

farm

shark

Tricky words

These tricky words are in the story you have just read. They cannot be sounded out. Can you memorize them and read them super fast?

he   into

all   you

the

Written by Claire Smith
Illustrated by Dean Gray

Barn Owl looks in the box.
He sees a cap, boots and
a big fork.

Barn Owl is a farmer!

I can dig the soil. I can pull up the turnips.

Barn Owl looks in the box.

He sees red shorts and a top.

Barn Owl is a surfer!

Barn Owl sees a cook's hat
and a jar of jam in the box.

Owl Chick sees the box.

Owl Chick looks in the box.

I can be
a queen . . .

. . . or
a singer!

Barn Owl is back.

Look at all this mess!

Barn Owl looks in the box.
He sees a monster!

Owl Chick!

Rar!

Story words

Can you match these words to the pictures?

fork

soil

surfer

jar

singer

monster